This is Footballer Fabio. He is
Story Town United's best striker.

A catalogue record for this book is available from the British Library

Published by Ladybird Books Ltd
80 Strand London WC2R 0RL
A Penguin Company

2 4 6 8 10 9 7 5 3 1

© LADYBIRD BOOKS LTD MMIV

Illustrations © Emma Dodd MMIV

LADYBIRD and the device of a Ladybird are trademarks of Ladybird Books Ltd

Little Workmates

Footballer Fabio

by Ronne Randall
illustrated by Emma Dodd

"Here we go! Here we go! Here we go!" said Footballer Fabio as he arrived at Story Town United Stadium.

Fabio was very excited. In the afternoon, he would be playing in the Cup Final against Littleville Wanderers!

Out on the pitch, Footballer Fabio practised his skills before the big game.

First, he practised penalty-shooting with Goalkeeper Gary. Then he and his teammates, Johnny and Mark, practised dribbling and passing and moving.

"Nice work!" called Coach Ken from the sideline.

After practice, the players went to the changing room to get ready for the match.

Footballer Fabio put on his shin pads, his stripy Story Town United socks and his lucky red football boots.

Out in the stadium, fans filled the stands.

Teacher Tina and Postman Pete wore their Story Town United scarves.

Truckdriver Tom and Mr Butcher waved a banner.

"Here we go!" everyone shouted as the Story Town United team ran out onto the pitch.

"Wheeeeeee!" The referee blew his whistle. Kick-off!

Johnny passed the ball to Fabio. Fabio raced towards the Littleville goal, past one player, past another.
Then – GOAL!

"Here we go! Here we go! Here we go!" sang the crowd.

The score was one-nil to Story Town United.

But, before the crowd had stopped celebrating, the Littleville goalkeeper kicked the ball right up to the other end of the pitch.

Oh no! The Littleville striker had scored a goal, too!

"Wheeeeeee!" went the referee's whistle.

It was half-time and the score was one-all!

Back in the changing room, Coach Ken passed oranges to the players.

"We need a goal to win the match," he said. "Fabio, you're our star striker. We're counting on you!"

"I'll do it, Coach!" said Fabio.

The second half began.

"Come on, Story Town!" called the crowd.

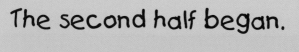

Mark passed the ball to Johnny. But – oh, no! Johnny fell and twisted his ankle!

Doctor Daisy rushed out to help Johnny. He would have to miss the rest of the game.

Coach Ken sent on a substitute, Dan.

The clock started ticking again. Would Fabio have time to score?

Dan dribbled and passed to Fabio.

Fabio shot. The ball went right in the back of the net! GOAL!

"Wheeeeeee!" The referee blew his whistle. Full-time!

The crowd roared. Story Town United had won the match two-one.

Queen Clara presented the team with the Cup.

Footballer Fabio held it high above his head and everyone cheered.

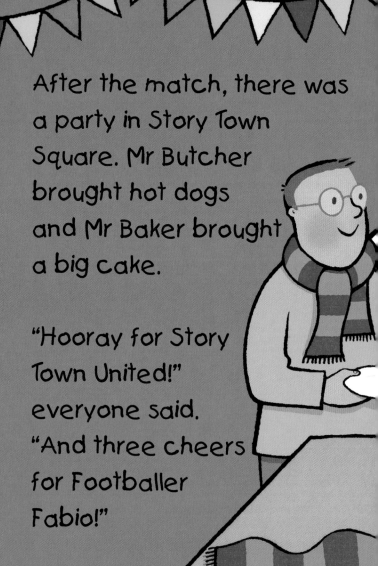

After the match, there was a party in Story Town Square. Mr Butcher brought hot dogs and Mr Baker brought a big cake.

"Hooray for Story Town United!" everyone said. "And three cheers for Footballer Fabio!"

Vet Vicky

Footballer Fabio

Builder Bill

Doctor Daisy

Fireman Fergus

Postman Pete

Nurse Nancy